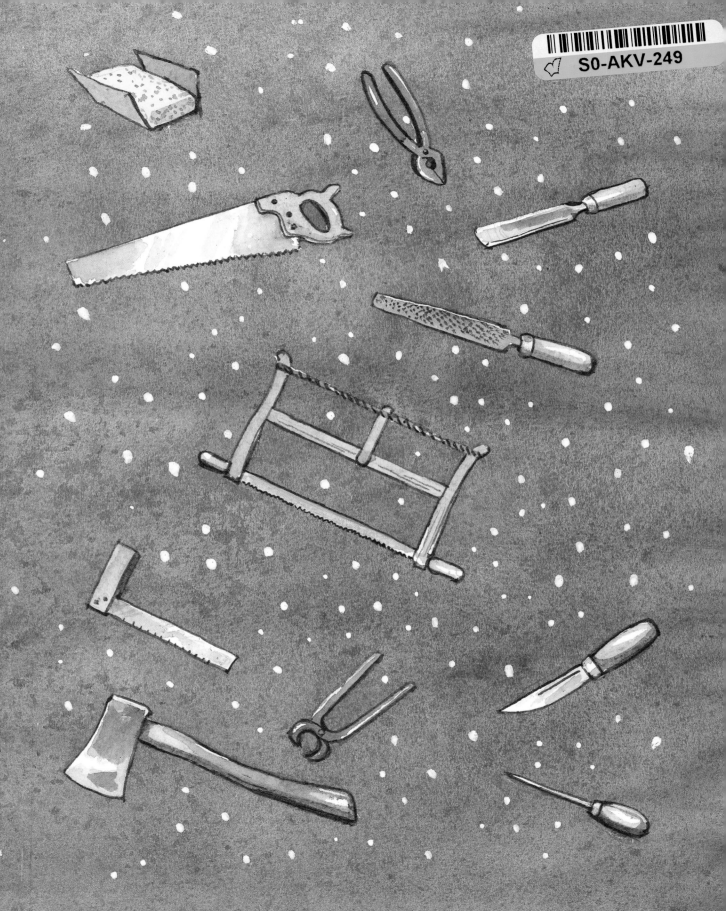

Christmas Eve
at Santa's

Rabén & Sjögren Stockholm

Pictures copyright © 1991 by Jens Ahlbom
Originally published in Sweden by Rabén & Sjögren under the title
Snickar Andersson och Jultomten, text copyright © 1971 by Alf Prøysen
Library of Congress catalog card number: 91-42059
Printed in Singapore
First edition, 1992

ISBN 91 29 62066 X

Christmas Eve at Santa's

ALF PRØYSEN AND JENS AHLBOM

Translated by Richard E. Fisher

R&S
BOOKS

Stockholm   New York   London   Adelaide   Toronto

Once there was a father called Carpenter Anderson. He had a lot of children, as fathers sometimes do. One Christmas Eve, he quietly slipped out of the house while his wife and his children sat around the table cracking nuts and playing games.

He went down to the woodshed, where he had hidden a
Santa Claus suit and a sled loaded with a big sack full of
Christmas presents. Carpenter Anderson put on the
costume and pulled the sled out into the yard.

But that Christmas Eve it was so icy that Carpenter Anderson slipped and fell, right on top of the sled—and the presents. The driveway sloped down out of the yard toward the road, and away slid the sled, with Carpenter Anderson and the presents! Another man in a Santa suit was coming up the road.

"Watch out!" yelled Carpenter Anderson, and tried to steer out of the way. But he couldn't see very well with the Santa mask on, and boom—with a great bump, they both tumbled into the ditch.

"Oh, excuse me!" said Carpenter Anderson.

"Excuse *me*," said the other man.

"We seem to have had the same idea," said Carpenter Anderson. "I see you've got your Santa suit on, too." He put out his hand and introduced himself: "Carpenter Anderson."

"Santa Claus," said the other man, and shook hands.

"Anything you say. It's good to make a joke or two on Christmas Eve," Carpenter Anderson said, laughing.

"Absolutely," said the other man. "If you agree, I'll go and give your children their Christmas presents, and you can visit mine. But you'll have to take off that silly Santa suit."

"How will I dress up, then?" asked Carpenter Anderson.

"You don't have to dress up. My children see elves all year long, but they have never seen a real carpenter. Every Christmas I say to them, 'If you are really good, Carpenter Anderson will come on Christmas Eve while I'm out taking presents to all the human children.' But this is the first time I've ever run into you—well, you ran into me. Why don't we do it tonight? Then my children won't have to be alone on Christmas Eve."

"Okay," said Carpenter Anderson, "but I don't have any presents for your children."

"Presents?" said Santa. "Aren't you a carpenter?"

"Well, yes," said Carpenter Anderson.

"Just take along some pieces of wood and some nails. You've got a knife, haven't you?"

Of course, Carpenter Anderson had a knife. And there were pieces of wood and nails in the woodshed.

"Now follow my tracks straight into the woods," said Santa, "and I'll take the sled and the sack and knock on your door. That's your house up there, isn't it?"

So Santa Claus headed for the carpenter's house. Carpenter Anderson followed Santa's tracks into the woods. He didn't have to go far. Just past a couple of spruces and a big stone, three little knitted caps stuck up behind a stump.

"Here he comes, here he comes," said three elf children, and raced off toward a blown-down spruce tree that lay with its roots in the air. When Carpenter Anderson got to the other side of the roots, there stood Santa's wife and the elf children, waiting for him.

"Here he comes, Mama! Here comes Carpenter Anderson! Look at him! See how tall he is!"

"Now, now, calm down, children," said Mrs. Santa. "You sound as if you'd never seen people before."

"We've never seen a real carpenter before!" yelled the children. "Come right in, Mr. Anderson!"

"Yes, please, do come in," said Mrs. Santa, and lifted up a branch. Carpenter Anderson stooped and followed them into a cozy room with a cobblestone floor and little chairs made out of stumps and little beds with lingonberry boughs as comforters. A little elf baby lay in the smallest bed, and an old elf grandpa sat in a corner, nodding his head.

"Have you got your knife with you? Have you got wood and nails?"

The children were all begging and pulling and tugging on Carpenter Anderson.

"Now, now, let Carpenter Anderson get inside the door," said Mrs. Santa. "Have a seat, Mr. Anderson!"

"What's this, a stranger?" croaked the old elf in the corner.

"This is Carpenter Anderson!" shouted the biggest elf boy into the old elf's ear horn.

"Our grandpa is so old he never gets out anymore. He'll be very pleased if you go over and say hello to him." Carpenter Anderson went over and shook Grandpa Elf's hand. It was like taking hold of a piece of bark.

"Now sit down, Mr. Anderson," said the children.

"Will you make a sled for me?" asked the biggest elf boy.

"I can try," said Carpenter Anderson. And in no time the sled was finished.

"Me next," said the second biggest elf child.

"What would you like?" asked Carpenter Anderson.

"A doll's bed," said the elf girl.

"Have you got a doll?" asked Carpenter Anderson.

"No, but I get to borrow the wood mouse's babies sometimes," said the elf girl. "And I can play with the baby squirrels as much as I like. They think it's fun to play dolls. Now please make a bed!"

Carpenter Anderson built a doll's bed.

"What would you like?" he said to the littlest child, who just stood there looking shy.

"I don't know," whispered the boy.

"He does, too," said the other children. "He knew earlier today. Say it!" they said to their brother.

"A top," whispered the littlest elf boy.

"A top it shall be!" said Carpenter Anderson, and he made a top.

"Now you have to make a present for Mama," said the
children. Mrs. Santa was hiding something behind her
back.

"You be quiet, children," she said.

"Just tell me what you'd like," said Carpenter Anderson.

Mrs. Santa showed him what she was hiding behind her
back. It was a wooden ladle. It was old, and cracked, and
full of splinters, so it was just about useless.

"Could you fix this, do you think?"

"Hmm," said Carpenter Anderson, and scratched his head. "I believe I'll carve a new ladle, instead."

He went out and found a nice root in the woods and carved a ladle. When he had finished it, he went back out and got a long, straight root that was bent at one end and began to carve it.

The children asked over and over what it was going to be, but he didn't say a word until he was done and the root had become a beautiful walking stick.

"There you are, Grandpa!"
shouted Carpenter Anderson,
and handed the cane to the old
elf grandpa.

And last but not least, he
picked up some shavings and
turned them into a little swallow
and hung it over the baby elf's
bed.

"You are much too kind!" said Mrs. Santa. "Thank you very much, Mr. Anderson. Children, thank nice Mr. Anderson! We will never forget this Christmas Eve!"

"Thank you, thank you, thank you!" shouted all the elf children. Grandpa Elf came toddling across the floor and said, "Many, many thanks indeed, young man!" Just then, Carpenter Anderson heard someone stamping outside, so he bowed and said, "Thank *you*, and Happy New Year!"

He hurried out. There stood Santa Claus with the sled
and an empty sack.

"Thanks for the help, Mr. Anderson," said Santa. "What
did the children say when you came?"

"Oh, they were happy. What about you? I hope my
littlest boy wasn't scared of you?"

"No, no," said Santa. "He thought I was you. He kept on
saying, 'Sit in lap, Daddy!'"

"Well, I'd better get on home," said Carpenter Anderson.
It had begun to snow, and he could just
barely see Santa's tracks.

"Can I see your Christmas presents?" he said to his children when he got to his house. They just laughed.

"You've seen them before!" they shouted. "You saw them when you were playing Santa Claus a few minutes ago!"

"No, no. I went to see the elf children and gave them some Christmas presents," said Carpenter Anderson.

"And where do they live?" asked the children, and laughed even more.

"Right over there, just a little way into the woods," said Carpenter Anderson, pointing.

It was snowing harder and harder — and before long,
there was no sign of the tracks left by Carpenter Anderson
and Santa Claus.

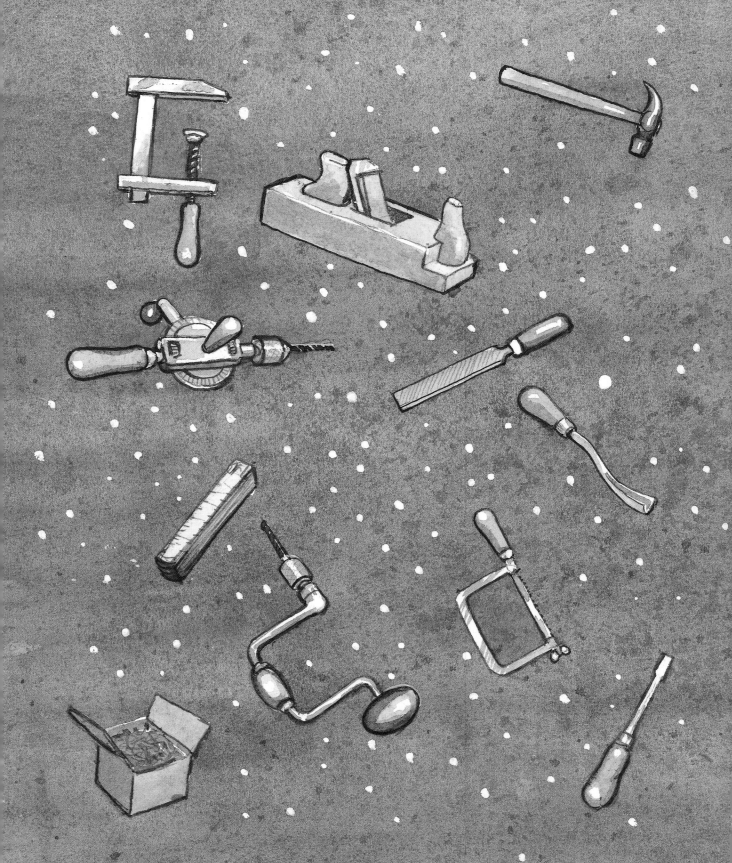